The Joke's on George

The Joke's on George

MICHAEL O. TUNNELL   pictures by KATHY OSBORN

For Adam, my friend
and neighbor
Welcome to Mr. Peale's world.
Please watch your step!
Happy reading
Michael O. Tunnell
10-11-93

TAMBOURINE BOOKS ● NEW YORK

Tambourine Books, a division of William Morrow & Company, Inc.,
1350 Avenue of the Americas, New York, New York 10019.
Printed in the United States of America.

Library of Congress Cataloging in Publication Data

Tunnell, Michael O.   The joke's on George / by Michael O. Tunnell:
illustrated by Kathy Osborn.–1st ed. p.cm.
Summary: Briefly surveys the life of the early American portrait
painter and describes an incident in which George Washington,
visiting his natural history museum, was fooled by a lifelike
painting of two of Peale's sons climbing a staircase.
1. Peale, Charles Willson, 1741-1827–Juvenile literature.
[1. Peale, Charles Willson, 1741-1827. 2. Artists. 3. Washington,
George, 1732-1799.] I. Osborn, Kathy, ill.   II. Title.
ND1329.P413T85 1993 759.13–dc20 [B] 92-33312 CIP AC
ISBN 0-688-11758-9 (trade).–ISBN 0-688-11759-7 (lib. bdg.)
1 3 5 7 9 10 8 6 4 2
First edition

To Glenna, who tried to climb those stairs   M.O.T.

To Paul and Lorie   K.O.

President George Washington had a reputation for being particularly polite. He doffed his hat to common servants and to fine gentlemen alike. Though such behavior was one of the many reasons that my family greatly admired Mr. Washington, there came a time when the President's politeness became a laughing matter.

One day, his old friend, Mr. Charles Willson Peale, invited George to visit a new display at Charles's world famous natural history museum. Of course, George said yes. But it was out of more than politeness and friendship that he accepted the invitation. I am sure that he was also a bit curious. Like most of us in Philadelphia, the President knew that Mr. Peale didn't do things in a normal, run-of-the-mill way. Never had, never would.

For instance, when his first pocket watch stopped working, did he take it to someone to be repaired? Certainly not. Charles just pulled his watch apart, studied how it worked, and fixed it himself. And when he saw portraits painted by Mr. Frazier from Norfolk, which he thought were terrible, Charles was convinced he could do a better job. Did it matter that he had never painted? Of course not. By the time Charles joined the American Revolution, a few years later, he had become one of America's best portrait painters. In fact, he painted more portraits of George Washington than any other artist.

Charles was an inventor, too, like his friend Benjamin Franklin. He designed bridges, experimented with new ways to heat houses, and built several devices that made life easier for folks, such as an apple parer and a corn husker. But some of his inventions were simply for fun, like the amazing moving picture theater. By shining lights from behind a transparent screen and moving objects on stage like puppets, Charles created exciting performances. One of the most popular was a naval battle using flashing lights for cannon fire and wooden waves that heaved up and down while water sprayed the audience from hidden pipes.

But it was Charles Willson Peale's Philadelphia Museum that we all thought
was the most amazing. Visitors never knew what strange and wonderful things to
expect. Its yard was a zoo filled with monkeys, eagles, bears, and snakes! Some

animals were in cages, but others, like a great elk and a strange five-legged, two-tailed cow, wandered about freely.

Inside, the museum was one of a kind, just like its curator. Not only were
Charles's famous portraits hung here and there, but there were displays filled
with stuffed animals, many peering at visitors from behind trees, rocks, and

grass. Never before had museum animals been displayed this way! And there
were glass cases of dried insects. And minerals and rocks. And even the gigantic
bones of a mysterious beast that Mr. Peale and other naturalists called a mammoth.

I believe President Washington couldn't help but smile as he thought about Charles Willson Peale. After all, the man didn't even give his children biblical names the way other God-fearing American colonists had. Most of his seventeen children were named after famous artists, names he'd found in a dictionary about painters: Raphaelle, Angelica Kauffmann, Rembrandt, Titian Ramsay, Rubens, Sophonisba Angusciola. Most people figured that Charles had chosen those names because he was so serious about his painting and George knew that was true. But he also knew that Mr. Peale had a sense of humor.

So, President George Washington was excited about seeing Mr. Peale's new display. He was about to retire and would soon return home to Mount Vernon, so it might be his last chance to visit Peale's Museum. Besides, going would be a nice break from the difficult job of being President.

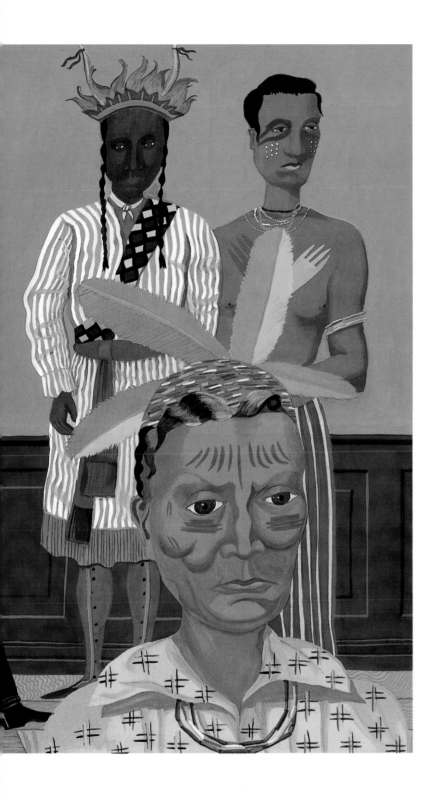

The new display was inspired by the Indian chiefs who often visited Philadelphia while it was America's capital. Mr. Peale had carefully fashioned wax figures of Chief Blue Jacket and his friend Red Pole of the Shawnee tribe. Then he added figures of people from several other world cultures. The rumor was that all the figures were dressed in authentic clothing and looked real enough to speak. So the President donned his hat and set off to inspect them. But little did George know that he was about to be fooled! Hoodwinked! Tricked! Right there in his friend's museum.

When George arrived, he and Charles ambled through the museum catching up on old times. Because there was always plenty to see, George was glancing this way and that as they strolled toward the wax figures. But then they drew near a door that led to a winding staircase. George slowed as he saw two familiar faces. Titian and Raphaelle Peale were just starting up the steps. Polite as always, President Washington smiled and bowed to the young men.

Then the slight smile on the President's face faded. Titian and Raphaelle hadn't bothered to return a greeting from the President of the United States— or worse, from their father's friend. In fact, they continued to ignore him completely!

Suddenly, Mr. Peale started to laugh. George Washington, the most respected man in America, was shocked that Charles seemed to think his sons' impudence amusing. The President was flummoxed, confused, dismayed—that is, until he noticed that Titian and Raphaelle hadn't moved a hair since he'd first spotted them. Then George Washington laughed too.

What George was looking at was the most incredible painting Mr. Peale would ever do. Its frame was a real doorjamb, and a wooden step extended the painted stairway out into the room. It was an illusion and a colossal joke! "Do not feel embarrassed," Charles said to George, "for not long ago a sharp-eyed dog tried to climb that staircase."

George Washington was expecting live-looking wax Indians. But he found live-looking oil-painted Peales, and his reputation for politeness was confirmed. Not many men would bow courteously to a painting!

I know this story is true, not because I heard it from a trustworthy source but because I was there. I am Rembrandt Peale, and the Philadelphia Museum was my home. By the way I saw more than one dog try to run up those stairs!

AUTHOR'S NOTE

The events in this story are, for the most part, true. Mr. Peale really accomplished all those amazing things, and more, during his lifetime. George Washington really was fooled by the painting called *The Staircase Group*, as were a few dogs. And Rembrandt Peale, who at age seventeen also painted a portrait of George Washington, was present when these events occurred. Later in his life, Rembrandt wrote about George Washington's habitual politeness, including doffing his hat to slaves and bowing to a portrait, but he did not elaborate as much as I have in this story. Therefore, it is difficult to know exactly what George and Charles said to one another that day or even if the events happened exactly the way that I've recreated them. After all, some of history always remains a mystery!